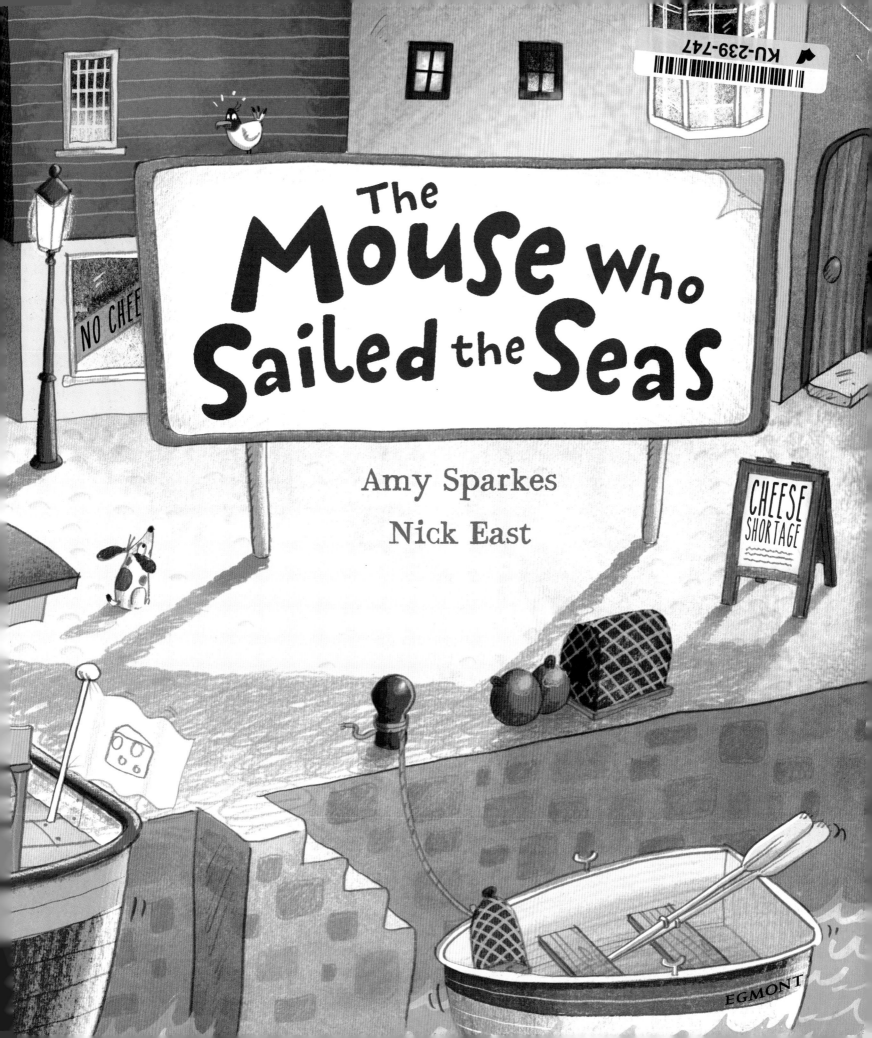

The MOUSE Who Sailed the Seas

Amy Sparkes

Nick East

NO CHEE[SE]

CHEESE SHORTAGE

EGMONT

THREE
LOST
BEES

A mouse he went to sail the seas.
He sailed the seas
    to look for cheese,
But all he found were . . .

Bumblebees!

A mouse he went
to sail the seas.
He sailed the seas to
look for **cheese**,
But all he found
were bumblebees

And . . .

Aliens like **purple peas!**

A mouse he went to sail the seas.
He sailed the seas to look for **cheese,**

But all he found were bumblebees
And aliens like purple peas
And . . .

Goats with very hairy knees!

A mouse he went to sail the seas.
He sailed the seas to look for cheese,

But all he found were bumblebees
And aliens like purple peas
And goats with very hairy knees
And . . .

Elves who had a magic sneeze!

AAAAACHOOOOO!

Now, a boat that's
on a quest for cheese,
Piled up high with **bumblebees**

And **aliens**
like purple peas

And **goats** with very hairy knees

And **elves** who had a magic sneeze . . .

AAAAAAACHOOOOOO!

Cannot sail the seas with ease.

There came a noisy,
    groaning CREAK!
The mouse let out
    a worried SQUEAK!
For now the boat
    began to LEAK!

The elves let out
a magic sneeze . . .

The goats with very hairy knees
Nibbled through their ropes with ease.
While the aliens like purple peas ...

Saved the mouse
who searched for cheese.

Then pulled up by the bumblebees,
Mouse floated high above the seas . . .

Beyond the sky, above the breeze,
He sailed up into space with ease.

Until he found . . .

A land of cheese!